Ali *and* *the* Spider

by Rowaa El-Magazy
illustrated by Stevan Stratford

Note: This book uses the name Allah and God interchangeably to mean the One Eternal God, Lord and Creator of the Universe.

ﷺ *Sallallahualayhi wa sallam* means 'Allah's blessing and peace be upon him.'

THE ISLAMIC FOUNDATION

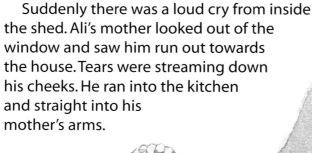

It was a lovely day. Ali was playing in the garden. The birds were singing and the sun was shining. Ali could see his mother in the kitchen washing the dishes. Through the open window he could hear her reciting the Qur'an. Ali saw that the door of the shed was open. He went inside.

Suddenly there was a loud cry from inside the shed. Ali's mother looked out of the window and saw him run out towards the house. Tears were streaming down his cheeks. He ran into the kitchen and straight into his mother's arms.

"*La hawla wala quwwata illa billah* (strength and power only belong to Allah), Ali! What's happened?" asked his mother. "What's the matter?"

"A spider! A big spider! I was in the shed looking for some toys and saw a spider in my toy box," sobbed Ali. "I hate spiders. They are no use to anyone. I just wish there were none in the world."

Ali's mother gave him a glass of water and a big hug. "Now calm down dear! Let's go and sit in the living room!"

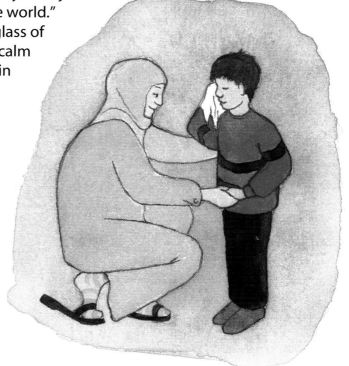

Ali sat beside his mother and she dried his tears. Then, she put her arm around him and began to tell him the following story.

A long time ago Prophet Muhammad ﷺ, began to teach the people of Makka how to become Muslims. He wanted them to worship only Allah, to be kind and help others.

After working with the people of Makka for thirteen years, there was little change. Although many people became Muslims, there were still a lot of people who refused to accept the Prophet's ﷺ kind words. They hurt the Muslims and became their enemies.

Allah told the Muslims of Makka that it was time to leave and go to Madina. Many people of Madina had already become Muslims and the people of Makka could live safely and peacefully with them.

The Muslims of Makka left in small groups. When they arrived in Madina, the people of Madina were really pleased to see them. Prophet Muhammad ﷺ stayed in Makka until all the Muslims had left for Madina.

Then, Allah told him to leave. So, one night, the Prophet ﷺ left Makka with his close friend Abu Bakr, before dawn, so as not to be seen.

The journey was difficult. After some time, they reached a cave called Thawr in which they stopped to rest."

"How did they keep safe while they were in the cave?" asked Ali, feeling a little shiver go down his back at the thought of the cold dark cave.

"Abu Bakr blocked up all the holes he could see, using his bare hands."

"That sounds really dangerous," said Ali. "There might have been snakes and scorpions inside the cave, or sss...spiders even!"
"Yes, there might have been," replied his mother, "but Abu Bakr didn't want anything to hurt the Prophet ﷺ."

"**A**bu Bakr must have loved the Prophet ﷺ more than anyone in the whole world," said Ali.

"Oh, yes he did, and his love of Allah was even greater. Abu Bakr was the Prophet's ﷺ best friend, and the first man to believe his message. We should all try and love the Prophet ﷺ as much as Abu Bakr did."

"**M**um," said Ali thoughtfully, "they hid in the cave, but how could they hide their tracks?"

"Well," said his mother, "before Abu Bakr left Makka, he asked his son to take his herd of sheep close to the cave where they were going to hide. The sheep would then cover their tracks. Allah protected His beloved messenger ﷺ and his friend.

Allah then told a pigeon and a spider to help. The pigeon was to build a nest outside the cave .The spider was to spin a web. In no time at all the pigeon built a beautiful nest of twigs and branches and laid its eggs inside. The spider wove a huge web that covered the entrance to the cave. Who could guess that two people had just got inside?

Although the Prophet ﷺ and Abu Bakr did their best to hide, their enemies hired some very good scouts and trackers and promised them a good reward. These were men of the desert who knew every broken twig and could spot the signs of movement of every living creature. Before long, the scouts had found the tracks leading to the Prophet's ﷺ hiding place. They crept up to the entrance of the cave. When they saw the spider's web and the pigeon's nest, they thought there was no need to look any closer. Birds and spiders never build their homes that close to human beings. Besides, if anyone had got in recently, they would have broken the web."

"*S*ubhan Allah! (Glory be to God). That's amazing," said Ali. "What happened next?"

"The Prophet ﷺ and his friend stayed in the cave for three days. Then, they continued their journey to Madina under Allah's protection. The joyful news of their arrival soon spread throughout the city. People quickly gathered to meet and greet the Prophet ﷺ and his trusted friend whom they all loved dearly. This was the start of a new and much safer life for the Prophet ﷺ and the Muslims."

Ali looked up with a big smile on his face. "That's a brilliant story. The spider helped to save the Prophet's ﷺ life! Spiders do scare me the way they rush about but I will try my best not to be frightened of them again."

"Would you like to go to the library tomorrow to learn more about spiders?" asked his mother.

"Yes please," replied Ali. "I would really like that."

The next day, Ali and his mother set off early to the library to learn more about Allah's creatures. Ali's mother whispered to him that they had to be quiet so that other people could read in peace. She taught him to say the prayer *"Rabbi zidni ilma"* which means, "O! My Lord, increase my knowledge."

Ali looked excitedly at the pictures of spiders of every shape and colour. He learnt that many different types of spiders could be found all over the world. More than 35,000! He wondered what kind of spider had helped to save the Prophet's ﷺ life.

Ali was happy to learn that most of the spiders found in our gardens are not harmful. In fact, many are very helpful. They eat flies and other insects which spread disease to human beings and farm crops.

"Spiders help keep balance on the Earth," said his mother. "Not only do they eat insects, but they are food for other animals such as birds and wasps.

Did you know that eye doctors sometimes use spider silk in their instruments to help people see better?"

"Really!" said Ali. "*Masha Allah!* (By the Will of Allah!)"

"Not only that, but the Qur'an tells us that spiders and other creatures praise Allah and glorify Him in their own special language."

"**W**ell, I am amazed!," Ali thought to himself. "These tiny creatures are full of surprises and do truly wonderful things."

"Mummy," he asked as they got ready to leave the library. "Would you buy me a magnifying glass?"

"What for?" asked his mother as she pushed the chairs back under the table.

"I think I'd like to take a really close look at some spiders' webs," replied Ali.

His mother looked at him and smiled. "There's a toy shop on the way home. Let's go and see if they have one for sale."

Spiders have eight legs.

They are not insects.

They are meat eaters (carnivores). They eat bugs, butterflies and insects.

Most spiders use a web to catch their prey.

It often takes about 20 minutes for a spider to spin its web.

Webs can usually be found in the early morning.

The female spins a yellow cocoon for her eggs.

She lays about 600–800 eggs.

Baby spiders are called spiderlings.

The bird-eating spiders of South America
are some of the largest in the world.

The Australian funnel web spider
is dangerous to humans.

Spiders belong to a group of creatures
called arachnids.